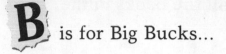 **B** is for Big Bucks...

The detective looked at the three friends.

"Tell you what," he said. "If you find the kid who filmed the robber, get the video. There'll be a nice reward if you hand it over."

"How much?" Josh asked.

"How about one hundred dollars for each of you?"

"A HUNDRED BUCKS?" screamed Ruth Rose.

The detective pulled out a small pad and a pencil. He wrote something and ripped off the page.

"Here's my phone number. Call me if you get that video."

Dink closed the door behind Detective Reddy. He grinned at Josh and Ruth Rose. "A hundred bucks each! We're rich!"

Collect all the books in the

series!

The Absent Author

The Bald Bandit

This is for my mother, Marie Jeanne Roy
–R.R.

To Christopher, for being a great Dink
–J.S.G.

Text copyright © 1997 by Ron Roy.
Illustrations copyright © 1997 by John Steven Gurney.
All rights reserved under International and Pan-American Copyright Conventions.
Published in the United States by Random House, Inc., New York, and simultaneously
in Canada by Random House of Canada Limited, Toronto.

http://www.randomhouse.com/

Library of Congress Cataloging-in-Publication Data
Roy, Ron. The bald bandit / by Ron Roy ; illustrated by John Gurney.
   p. cm. — (A to Z mysteries) "A Stepping Stone book."
SUMMARY: Third-grader Dink and his detective friends hope to receive a big
reward by finding the person whose video recorder picked up a picture of the
local bank robber.
ISBN 0-679-88449-1 (pbk.) — ISBN 0-679-98449-6 (lib. bdg.)
[1. Mystery and detective stories.] I. Gurney, John, ill. II. Title.
III. Series: Roy, Ron. A to Z mysteries.
PZ7.R8139Bal 1997 [Fic]—dc21 96-40473

Printed in the United States of America   13 12 11 10 9 8 7 6 5

The
Bald
Bandit

by **Ron Roy**

illustrated by
John Steven Gurney

A STEPPING STONE BOOK™

Random House 🏠 New York

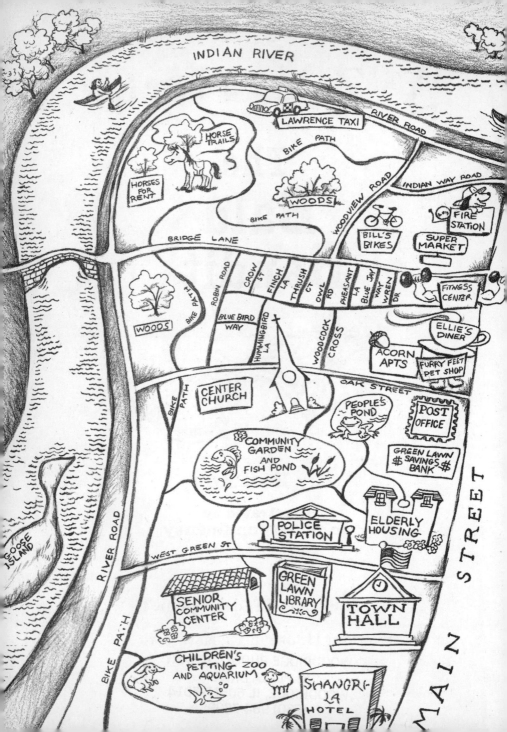

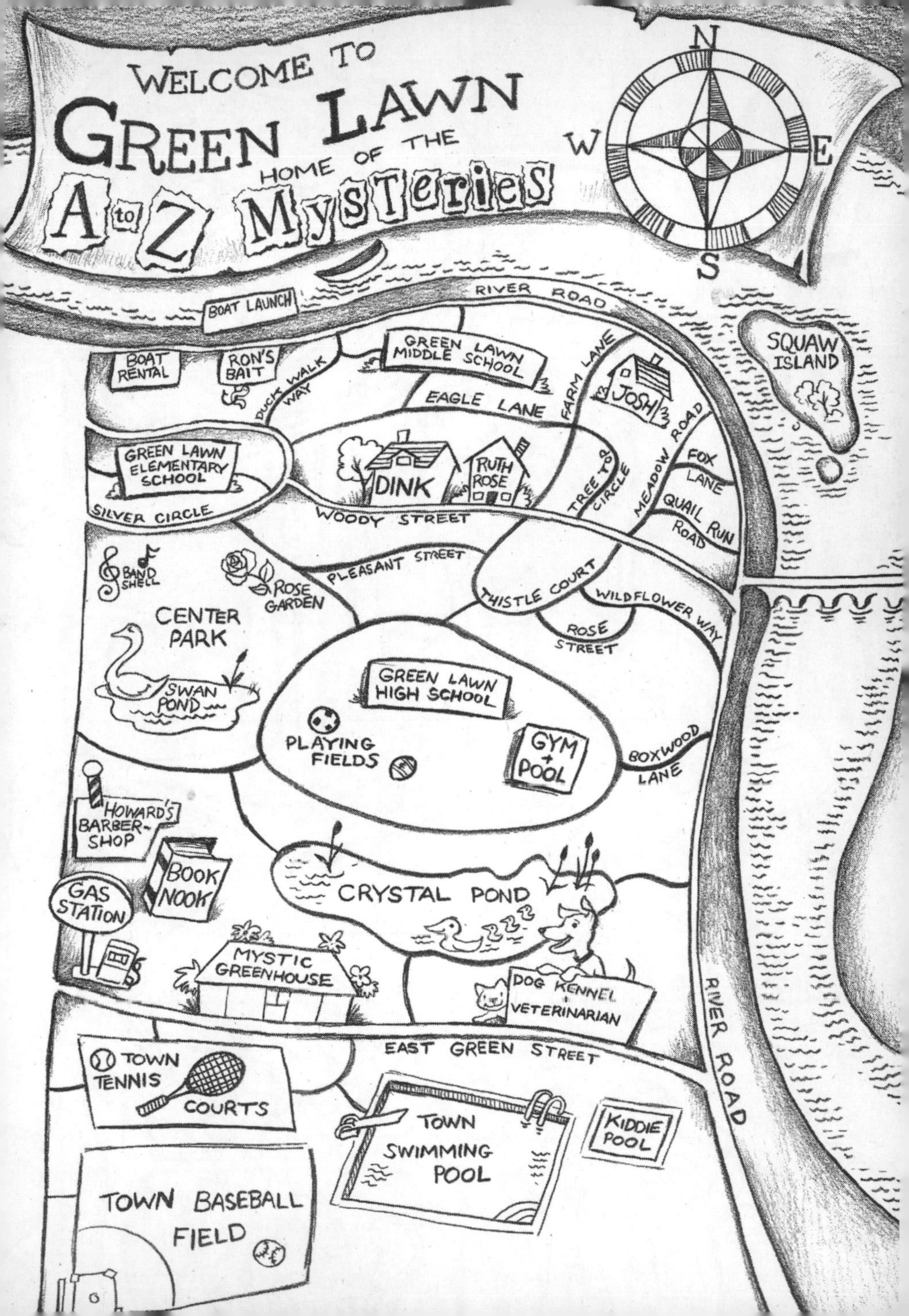
WELCOME TO
GREEN LAWN
HOME OF THE
A to Z Mysteries
N
S
E
W
BOAT LAUNCH
RIVER ROAD
SQUAW ISLAND
BOAT RENTAL
RON'S BAIT
DUCK WALK WAY
GREEN LAWN MIDDLE SCHOOL
FARM LANE
JOSH
EAGLE LANE
MEADOW ROAD
GREEN LAWN ELEMENTARY SCHOOL
DINK
RUTH ROSE
TREE TOP CIRCLE
FOX LANE
QUAIL RUN ROAD
SILVER CIRCLE
WOODY STREET
BAND SHELL
ROSE GARDEN
PLEASANT STREET
THISTLE COURT
WILDFLOWER WAY
CENTER PARK
ROSE STREET
SWAN POND
GREEN LAWN HIGH SCHOOL
PLAYING FIELDS
GYM + POOL
BOXWOOD LANE
HOWARD'S BARBER-SHOP
BOOK NOOK
GAS STATION
CRYSTAL POND
MYSTIC GREENHOUSE
DOG KENNEL + VETERINARIAN
RIVER ROAD
EAST GREEN STREET
TOWN TENNIS COURTS
TOWN SWIMMING POOL
KIDDIE POOL
TOWN BASEBALL FIELD

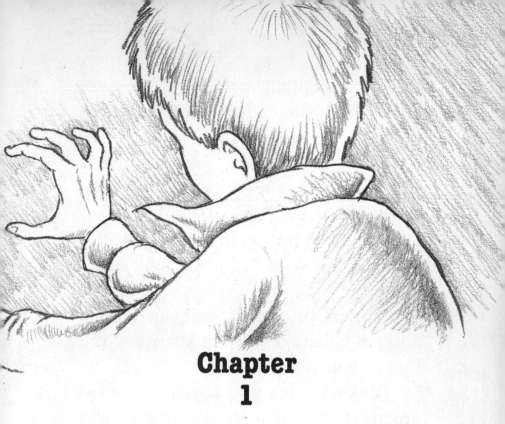

Chapter 1

Dink slipped the plastic fangs into his mouth. He made a scary face at his best friend, Josh Pinto.

"Do I look like a vampire?" It was hard to talk without spitting, so Dink took the fangs out again.

Dink's full name was Donald David Duncan, but nobody called him

Donald. Except his mom, when she was upset. Then she called him by all three names.

Josh grinned. "No. You look like a skinny third-grader wearing false teeth."

"Wait till I put on the rest of my costume," Dink said. "Then I'll look like a vampire."

"Maybe you will." Josh was tearing a green bedsheet into long strips. "And maybe you won't."

Dink's guinea pig, Loretta, crawled among the green strips. Every now and then she let out a curious squeak.

"How will you be able to walk if you're wrapped up in all those strips?" Dink asked Josh.

Josh kept tearing. "Swamp monsters don't walk," he said in a slithery voice. "They *gliiiide*."

"Okay, so how will you be able to

gliiiide wrapped up in all those strips?"

The doorbell rang. When Dink opened the door, his next-door neighbor, Ruth Rose, was standing on the steps.

"Hi, Ruth Rose. Why are you wearing a wig? Halloween isn't until tomorrow."

Ruth Rose was dressed in her usual bright clothes—a pink shirt, pink pants, and pink sneakers. But on her head she wore a shiny black wig. She also had on thick fake eyebrows.

Ruth Rose wiggled the fake eyebrows up and down. "Guess who I am!"

Josh stared at Ruth Rose. "A hairy princess?"

"No."

"Groucho Marx?"

She shook her head.

"Tell us, Ruth Rose," Dink said.

Ruth Rose pretended to strum a

guitar. "I'm Elvis!" she cried.

"That was my next guess," Josh said.

Ruth Rose looked at his mound of green strips. "What are you supposed to be?"

Josh wrapped a strip around his face. He made a swamp monster face at Ruth Rose.

"Guess," he said.

Ruth Rose smiled sweetly. "You're a green sheet torn into strips."

The doorbell rang again.

This time Dink saw a tall man standing on the doorstep. He was dressed in a suit and tie. He had dark curly hair, a droopy mustache, and a dimpled chin.

"Hi, there. My name is Detective Reddy. I was hired by the Green Lawn Savings Bank to find someone. Did you hear about the robbery?"

Josh and Ruth Rose came to the

door and stood behind Dink.

Dink nodded. "I heard about it on TV."

"Are you looking for the robber?" Josh asked.

Detective Reddy shook his head. "Right now I'm looking for someone who saw him. When the thief ran out of the bank, he took off his mask. Some kid was walking by with a video camera. He got the thief on tape. The bank hired me to find the kid so I can get the video."

"What does the kid look like?" Ruth Rose asked.

Detective Reddy stared at her Elvis wig. "Someone in the bank said he has red hair and he's tall and skinny."

"Sounds like you, Josh," said Dink. He laughed and pointed at Josh's red hair.

"It wasn't me, honest!" Josh said. "I

don't even have a video camera."

"No, the kid was a lot older than you," said the detective. "Probably in high school." He patted his mustache. "Do you guys know anyone like that?"

"No," Dink said. "But we do know Green Lawn pretty well. Maybe we can help you find him."

The detective looked at the three friends.

"Tell you what," he said. "Check the high school tomorrow. If you find the kid who filmed the robber, get the video. There'll be a nice reward if you hand it over."

"How much?" Josh asked.

"How about one hundred dollars for each of you?"

"A HUNDRED BUCKS?" screamed Ruth Rose.

Dink, Josh, and Detective Reddy covered their ears.

"Ouch!" said Detective Reddy. "That's quite a set of lungs you've got there."

"How can we get in touch with you if we find the kid?" Dink asked.

The detective pulled out a small pad and a pencil. He wrote something and ripped off the page.

"Here's my phone number. Call me if you get that video."

Dink closed the door behind Detective Reddy. He grinned at Josh and Ruth Rose. "A hundred bucks each! We're rich!"

Chapter 2

"Here's the plan," Dink said.

It was almost three o'clock the next afternoon. Dink, Josh, and Ruth Rose were headed for the high school, a few blocks away from Green Lawn Elementary.

"Josh, you cover the back door. Ruth Rose, your station is the bike rack. But keep an eye on the parking lot, too."

"How can I watch the bike rack *and* the parking lot?" asked Ruth Rose.

"Watch one with each eye," Josh said, grinning.

"What's your station?" Ruth Rose asked Dink.

"I'll be watching the front door. If anyone sees a skinny redhead, stop him and yell."

Ruth Rose laughed. "Stop him and yell? He'll think we're crazy and run away."

"She's right," Josh said.

Dink scratched his thick blond hair. "Hmm. Okay, don't yell. Just get his name and tell him he may have won some money."

They cut through the park next to the high school.

"What money?" Josh asked.

"Well, if Detective Reddy is going to pay us a hundred dollars each to find the video, I figure we can give the kid half the money. But only if he gives us the video."

At the high school, they split up.

Josh ran around to the back of the school. Ruth Rose sat on the lawn next to the bike rack.

Dink sat on a bench where he had a good view of the front door.

Suddenly, he heard a loud bell. Ten seconds later, the front door burst open. A million high school kids shoved

through the door and scrambled down the front steps.

Dink stood on the bench so he wouldn't get trampled. He was looking for red hair, but it wasn't easy to spot. Some of the kids had hats on. Some wore jackets or sweatshirts with the hoods pulled up. Sometimes Dink couldn't tell if a kid was a boy or a girl!

Finally, he spotted a tall guy with red hair. Dink jumped off the bench and ran after him.

"Excuse me," Dink said, trying to catch his breath.

"Who are you?" the redhead asked.

"Dink Duncan." Dink tried to remember his plan. "You may have won some money!"

The redhead stared down at Dink. "Money? Me? Why? How much money?"

"Were you near the bank when the

robbery happened last week?" he asked.

The kid kept staring at Dink. "Robbery? What robbery?"

"You didn't hear about it? It was on the news, on TV. Some guy robbed Green Lawn Savings Bank."

"So what's it to you?"

"A kid with red hair got the robber on tape," Dink said. "I'm helping to find him. There's going to be a reward."

"Rats, I wish I did tape the guy," the redhead said, shaking his head. "I could use a reward. But I wasn't anywhere near the bank last week." He waved and headed for the park. "Good luck!"

Dink looked around for another redhead, but everyone had disappeared.

He walked toward the bike rack. Ruth Rose was sitting on the lawn, weaving grass blades together.

"Did you see any redheads?" Dink

asked, plopping down beside her.

"Three," Ruth Rose said. "One was a short, fat boy. One was a girl. One was a teacher."

Josh came running up.

"Any luck?" he asked.

"Nope," Dink said. "How'd you do?"

"I talked to two guys with red hair. One of them told me to take a hike. The other one was an exchange student from Ireland. He told me i doesn't even know where the bank is."

"Great," Dink said. "We all struck out. Now what do we do?"

Josh tossed a pine cone at a tree. "Beats me."

"We should search the whole neighborhood," Ruth Rose said.

"How?" Dink asked.

Ruth Rose stood up and dusted off her shorts. "Easy. We just go door to door and ask."

"How can we do that without our parents finding out?" Josh asked. "Mine won't let me get involved with some bank robber, that's for sure."

"Mine either," Dink said.

"So how do we explain why we're wandering around Green Lawn knocking on everyone's doors?" asked Josh.

"Come on, guys," Ruth Rose said. "Think about it. What's tonight?"

Dink and Josh looked at each other. *"Halloween!"*

Chapter 3

With black shoe polish in his hair and plastic fangs in his mouth, Dink looked like Dracula.

His mom had made him a cape from an old black raincoat. He tied the cape around his neck just as the doorbell rang.

A strange creature stood on his porch. The thing was wrapped in green cloth. Tufts of red hair poked out at the top. Large black high-tops stuck out at the bottom.

"How do I look?" the thing asked.

Dink took out his fangs and grinned. "Like some weird vegetable. Half carrot and half asparagus."

Josh shuffled inside the house.

"You look pretty good, Dink. I like the blood dripping down your chin."

The bell dinged again. This time it was a miniature Elvis. Ruth Rose was wearing a white suit with sequins everywhere. She even carried a little guitar. Her Elvis wig made her look about two inches taller.

Ruth Rose strummed her guitar and wiggled her hips.

"Thank you very much, ladies and gentlemen," she said, taking a bow.

"Come on in, Elvis," Dink said. "We have to talk about Operation Redhead before we go trick-or-treating."

They sat at Dink's kitchen table. A basket of candy stood waiting for the neighborhood kids.

"Here's my plan," Dink said. "Every house we go to, we ask if anyone knows a skinny redheaded kid."

"That's *my* plan!" Ruth Rose said.

Dink grinned. "Oh, yeah, I forgot."

One of Ruth Rose's black eyebrows was crooked. "We have to keep our eyes peeled. Check out tall kids trick-or-treating."

"Got it," Dink said.

"Anyone with red hair, we ask them if they took a video of the bank robber," Ruth Rose went on.

"Check," Dink said. "Any other ideas?"

"Yeah, I got a great idea," Josh said. "Let's stop talking and get moving!"

Dink's mother walked into the kitchen. She screamed and clutched her chest.

"Oh, my goodness! Monsters in my kitchen!"

Ruth Rose stood up. "I'm not a monster, Mrs. Duncan. I'm Elvis!"

Dink's mom adjusted Ruth Rose's left eyebrow. "I know, honey. You make a great Elvis. But these other two!" She shuddered and made a terrified face.

"We're going now, Mom." Dink fit the plastic fangs over his teeth. He handed Josh a paper bag and took one for himself.

"Please be back in two hours," his mother said. "Dad and I will have some cider and doughnuts for you."

The three kids each took a different street. They agreed to meet back at Dink's house in about two hours.

Dink headed down Woody Street. He looked at every tall kid in a costume, checking for red hair. But most of the kids out were shorter than him. He counted seventeen ghosts, twenty little witches, eight angels with floppy wings, and a zillion small furry animals.

Dink rang Mrs. Davis's doorbell. "Trick or treat!"

"Oh, hello, Dink!" said Mrs. Davis. She dropped a small bag of candy kisses into his sack.

"Have you seen any redheaded kids tonight?" Dink asked.

"Redheads?" Mrs. Davis patted her white hair. "I'm afraid I don't know anyone besides your friend Josh who has red hair."

Dink thanked Mrs. Davis for the candy and walked next door to old Mr. Kramer's house.

Mr. Kramer was a little deaf.

"Do you know a skinny redhead?" asked Dink in a loud voice.

Mr. Kramer turned one ear and leaned toward Dink. "What's that you say? A tinny red bed?"

"A skinny red*head!*" Dink yelled even louder. He wished he had Ruth Rose with him. She was the only one loud enough for Mr. Kramer to hear.

Mr. Kramer dropped a nickel in Dink's bag and slammed the door. Dink sighed.

He followed some ghosts to the next house on Woody Street.

A gorilla opened the door when Dink rang the bell. It had a hairy chest and a huge mouth filled with yellow teeth.

"Trick or treat!" said Dink.

The gorilla dropped a banana into Dink's bag.

"Have you seen any tall redheaded teenagers walking around?" Dink asked.

The gorilla grunted and shook his head.

"Thanks anyway," said Dink.

Two hours later, Dink, Josh, and Ruth Rose poured their candy onto Dink's dining room table.

Dink took out his fangs. "Any luck?" he asked.

Josh unwrapped his face. "I saw four redheads. Two girls about ten years old and two adults. No one I talked to knew a skinny redhead in high school."

Ruth Rose took off her wig and eyebrows and dropped them into her plastic jack-o'-lantern.

"Same here," she sighed, slumping in her chair. "Nobody knew the right redhead. And I asked everybody!"

Josh ripped open a miniature bag of M&M's.

"I really wanted that hundred bucks," he said. "Maybe we should just forget it."

"Give up after just two days? No way, you guys!" Dink climbed up on the table. He wrapped his cape around his face so just his eyes showed.

In his best Count Dracula voice, he said, *"Vee vill never giff up!"*

Chapter 4

The next morning, Dink's hair was stiff with black shoe polish. He shampooed three times before he got out of the shower.

The bathroom mirror was fogged up when he tried to see his reflection. He wiped the mirror, looked at himself, and gasped.

His hair wasn't its usual blond and it wasn't vampire black. It was a muddy brown color, like the rusty parts on his bike.

"Mom! Help!"

His mother peeked into the bathroom. "What's the...oh, I see." She giggled.

"It's not funny, Mom. How am I supposed to go outside like this? My hair looks like it rusted!"

"Honey, lots of kids will have traces of makeup on their faces or color in their hair today. It's the day after Halloween."

Dink rubbed a towel over his hair as hard as he could. He looked in the mirror. Now he had *frizzy* rust-colored hair.

"Be thankful it's Saturday," his mother said, smiling. "At least you don't have to go to school today."

After breakfast, Dink jammed his baseball cap over his hair and headed for Josh's house.

When Dink got there, Josh was already shooting hoops in front of his barn. He grinned at Dink.

"What's wrong with your hair?" he asked.

Dink yanked his hat off. "Take a look. The stupid shoe polish from last night won't wash out. I had to be a vampire, right? I couldn't just be a cowboy or an astronaut."

Josh dribbled and took a shot. He missed the hoop.

"So have you thought of a plan for finding that kid with the video?" Josh asked.

"No," said Dink, jamming his hat back over his hair.

"Well, what do we do now?" said Josh. "Ask at more houses?"

"I don't know," Dink said. "Now that Halloween is over, we'd look pretty suspicious. Besides, Green Lawn has hundreds of houses. We'd be knocking on doors for a month."

Josh made a perfect shot. "Two points!"

"We have to use our heads instead of our feet," Dink said, grabbing the ball after Josh's basket.

A door slammed behind them.

"Uh-oh," Josh mumbled.

"Josh, it's time to go," his mother called. "Come in and brush your teeth, please."

"I have a dentist appointment," Josh said. "Call me later, okay?"

"Okay." Dink tossed Josh's ball into the barn and started walking away.

"Hey!" Josh yelled behind him. "I think your new hair color looks just *adorable!*"

"Very funny," Dink muttered, tugging his hat down even tighter.

Maybe I'll cut my hair off, he thought. *Go to school bald on Monday.*

Suddenly, he stopped walking.

Thinking about cutting his hair off gave him an idea.

He ran toward Main Street. At Howard's Barbershop, he peered through the glass. Howard was watching an *I Love Lucy* rerun on a small TV set.

Dink walked in, setting off the sleigh bells hanging over the door. Whenever he came to Howard's for a haircut, Dink thought about Christmas.

"What'll it be today, Dink?" Howard asked. "Want a flattop? How about one of them Mohawk jobbies, with the stripe down the middle?"

"I don't want a haircut," Dink said. "I need to ask you something."

Howard squinted one blue eye. He lifted Dink's baseball cap. "What happened to your hair?"

Dink blushed. "I was a vampire last night. I used black shoe polish in my

hair and it won't come out. I tried."

Howard grinned. "Hop up in the chair, me lad. I'll dose you with me special shampoo. You can ask your question while I perform a little magic."

Dink hung his hat on a peg and

climbed into the barber chair. Howard
pulled a bottle and some white towels
out of a cupboard.

"I was wondering if you know any
kids with red hair," Dink said. "Besides
Josh."

Howard draped a towel around Dink's shoulders and pinned it in back. He misted Dink's hair with a spray bottle of water.

"I might," he answered. "Why, do you want me to dye your hair red?"

Dink laughed. "No, I'm looking for a certain kid who has red hair. I think he's a teenager."

"I know one teenager who *had* red hair," Howard said, pouring green shampoo onto Dink's hair. "But I shaved it all off last week. Came running in here all excited, out of breath. 'Shave my head!' he tells me. So I did."

The smell of the shampoo made Dink's eyes water. He felt his heart start to tap-dance.

"Was he carrying a video camera?" Dink asked.

Howard rubbed the shampoo into Dink's hair.

"Why all the questions about this redheaded boy?" he asked.

Dink thought for a few seconds, then decided to spill the beans. He told Howard about the bank robber, about the kid with the video camera, and about the three hundred dollars the detective had promised.

Howard chuckled. "Oh, now I see why the boy ran in here yelling for me to cut off all his hair. He didn't want the bank bandit to recognize him. So if I tell you this lad's name, you're going to persuade him to give you the videotape?"

"Yes, if I can," Dink said.

"What about the money?" said Howard.

Dink looked at Howard in the mirror. "What about it?"

"Would you be planning to share the reward with the redheaded boy?"

Dink grinned. "Sure. We'll give him

half of what we get from the detective."

"That sounds like a fine idea." Howard rubbed Dink's hair vigorously. Dink watched in the mirror. His hair was a slimy green mess.

"Does this stuff really get shoe polish out?" he asked.

"Yup. Invented it meself," Howard said. "Secret recipe. I used it once to get bubble gum out of me granddaughter's hair. It took tar out of our dog's fur, too."

Howard swung the barber chair around and lowered its back. He positioned Dink's head over the sink.

"Close your eyes, me boy. Let's wash this gook out and see what's what."

Dink liked the feel of the warm water and Howard's fingers smoothing the shampoo out of his hair. After a few minutes, Howard sat him up and plopped a fresh towel on his head.

"Dry off. I think you're back to normal."

Dink rubbed his hair with the towel, then looked in the mirror. He laughed out loud. "You did it!"

Howard smiled at Dink's reflection. "I should sell this stuff and make a million dollars."

"How much do I owe you?" Dink asked.

"This one's on me, young fella. And the boy with red hair is Lucky O'Leary. He lives over on Robin Road with his mum and his little brothers and sisters. All six of 'em! Nice kids, and every last one's a redhead."

Howard grinned as he lowered the chair.

"Except for Lucky, who suddenly decided to go bald."

Chapter 5

"He's *bald?*" Josh said, climbing Ruth Rose's front steps.

Dink had run right home from the barbershop and called Josh. Now they were picking up Ruth Rose so they could go to Robin Road together.

"That's what Howard said," Dink told Josh. He pushed the doorbell.

"So that's why we didn't spot him at the high school!" Josh said.

"COME IN!" Ruth Rose screamed from inside.

Ruth Rose was sitting on the floor

watching a video with her four-year-old brother, Nate.

"Come on, Ruth Rose. I think we found the redhead!" Dink said. "We're going to his house."

Ruth Rose jumped up and screamed, "I'M LEAVING WITH THE GUYS, MOM! WATCH NATE!"

Dink and Josh covered their ears.

Ruth Rose told Nate, "You stay right here and wait for Mommy, okay?"

Nate nodded and kept his eyes on the TV set.

"Let's go." Ruth Rose led the way back to the door and skipped down the front steps.

"How'd you find the kid?" she asked.

Dink explained how he hadn't been able to get the shoe polish out of his hair.

"That made me think about cutting

my hair off. And *that* made me think about the barbershop. Who would know all the redheads in Green Lawn?"

"HOWARD THE BARBER!" she screamed.

The boys covered their ears again.

"I'm going to need a hearing aid like old Mr. Kramer," Josh muttered.

Dink had looked up O'Leary in the phone book to get the address on Robin Road. They stopped in front of house number 33. It was a big blue house with toys and bikes and sneakers and basketballs all over the lawn. Loud music came out through the front door.

They walked onto the porch and stepped over a baseball bat. Four pumpkins sat in a row, all carved with scary faces.

Dink rang the bell. "Keep your fingers crossed," he said.

A little girl opened the door. She

had red hair and a face full of freckles.

"Hi! I'm Josephine and I'm five and a half!" She held up ten fingers.

"Is your brother home?" Dink asked.

"Which one? I have this many!" Josephine held up ten fingers again.

Dink laughed. "Do you have a big brother named Lucky?"

The music went off.

"Who's out there, Jo?" a voice called. A tall, skinny teenager wearing torn jeans and a T-shirt came up behind Josephine. Dink noticed red fuzz covering his head, like a new red lawn.

"Are you Lucky O'Leary?" Dink asked.

The kid looked down at Dink and Josh and Ruth Rose. "Who wants to know?"

"We do," Ruth Rose said. "How'd you like to earn some money?"

"I might," he said.

"We're looking for a kid who got the Green Lawn bank robber on video last week," Dink said. "The bank hired a detective to find the video, and we're helping the detective. He's paying us to get the video, and we'll split the money with you. If you're the kid, I mean."

"Are you?" Ruth Rose asked.

The kid rubbed the top of his fuzzy red head. "Yeah," he muttered. "I'm the guy."

Then he crossed his arms. "But I'm not giving my tape to any detective."

Chapter 6

The kids stared at Lucky.

"Why not?" Ruth Rose asked. "The detective is helping the bank find the robber. You could be a HERO!"

"Shh!" said Lucky. He looked around nervously. Then he beckoned Dink, Josh, and Ruth Rose inside.

"Come on."

Inside Lucky's house, the kids followed him down a hallway into his bedroom. Dink noticed that he was limping. His room had posters of basketball players on the walls. There were clothes all over the floor.

Lucky flopped down on his bed.

"Listen," he said. "I'm afraid to give that tape to the detective. What if the robber found out I handed it over? With my luck, he'd come after me."

"How would the robber know it was you who taped him?" Dink asked.

Lucky sat up. "Because he looked right at me when he ran out of the bank. The guy saw me taping him! That's why I ran to Howard's to get my head shaved." Lucky scratched his fuzzy head.

"But if you turn in the tape, the robber will get caught. Then you won't have to worry about him at all," said Josh.

"Besides, we'll give you half of our reward," Ruth Rose said. "Right, guys?"

"Right," Dink said. "Is Lucky your real name?"

The kid shook his head. "It's Paul. Lucky is my nickname. People call me that because I always have such rotten luck. Since school started, my dog died, my bike got stolen, and I broke my toe. I can barely walk to school."

"You can buy a new bike with the reward money," Ruth Rose said. "Then you won't have to walk."

Lucky smiled at Ruth Rose. "I'm saving all my money for college," he said. Then he sighed. "It seems like I'll never get enough."

Lucky thought for a minute.

"Listen, that reward money would really help," he said. "But you guys have to *promise* not to tell who gave you the video."

They all nodded.

"Okay," said Lucky. He got off the bed and limped over to his closet. He pulled a box from the top shelf. The box

was filled with videotapes. He handed
one of the tapes to Dink.

Lucky looked embarrassed. "Um...

when can I get the money?" he asked.

"Maybe tomorrow," Dink said. "We'll let you know, okay?"

"Sure, that'll be fine," said Lucky. He pretended to zip his lips closed. "And remember, you promised not to tell anyone where you got the video. Not even that detective."

The kids nodded again.

Lucky walked them to the door, stepping around a pile of kids wrestling on the living room floor. Dink noticed they all had red hair and freckles.

Josephine popped up out of the pile.

"Bye!" she said, smiling at Dink.

As soon as they were on the sidewalk, Dink, Josh, and Ruth Rose triple-high-fived each other.

"We got it!" Josh yelled.

Dink slipped the tape into his pocket. "Now we just have to call Detective Reddy and get our money!"

Chapter 7

The kids hurried back to Dink's house. There was no one home. Dink opened the front door with his key.

He saw a note on the kitchen table.

DAD AND I ARE OUT SHOPPING. WE'LL BE BACK SOON. HAVE A SNACK. LOVE, MOM

Dink was glad his folks were out. He knew they wouldn't like him playing detective. When this was all over, he'd tell them how he earned the hundred bucks.

Josh opened Dink's refrigerator. "What do you have to eat?" he asked.

Dink set the tape on the counter. "There should be some doughnuts on the counter."

He pulled the paper with the detective's number on it out of his pocket. He called the number.

"Hello, is this Detective Reddy? This is Dink Duncan. Me and my friends found that video for you. What? No, we haven't looked at it. Okay. Bye."

Dink hung up smiling. "He'll be right over. He said we were good detectives. He told us not to look at the video."

Josh was eating a doughnut. "Why

not?" he said with his mouth full.

"He said it was top secret."

They all looked at each other.

"Come on!" Dink said, grabbing the video.

They ran into the living room. Dink turned on the TV and slid the tape into the VCR.

The first part of the video showed a big dog chewing on a rubber bone. Then they saw a girl in a bathing suit. She was laughing and running away from the camera. Next came a birthday party. Most of the people in the picture looked like Lucky O'Leary. Dink recognized little Josephine.

Finally, they saw the front of the Green Lawn Savings Bank. The door opened and a man came running out. He was pulling off a ski mask.

"That must be the robber!" Dink said. He pressed the pause button.

The man on the tape was completely bald. His head was shiny in the sunlight. He was wearing sweatpants and a sweatshirt, and he was carrying a gym bag. He had a surprised look on his face.

"That must be when he noticed Lucky taping him," Josh said.

Ruth Rose moved closer to the TV. "Look, he's got a dimple on his chin."

Suddenly, Ruth Rose gasped. She ran across the room and out of the house. The door slammed behind her.

Dink looked at Josh. "What's going on?"

Josh shrugged. "Maybe she doesn't like guys with dimples."

A minute later, the door burst open and Ruth Rose ran back in. She was carrying her Elvis wig and her fake eyebrows.

Ruth Rose stuck one eyebrow on the

TV screen, under the bandit's nose. It looked like a mustache. She held the wig over the bandit's bald head.

"Who does that look like?" she demanded.

Josh jumped into the air. "Oh, my gosh! The bank robber looks exactly

like Detective Reddy!"

Just then the doorbell rang. Dink peeked through the front window.

"Who is it?" Josh asked.

Dink's eyes were bugging out when he turned around. "It's Detective Reddy!"

Chapter 8

Ruth Rose snatched the wig and eyebrow off the TV and hid them behind her back.

Josh pushed the eject button and slid the video inside his shirt.

Dink stared at the door. He didn't think he could walk.

The bell rang again.

Dink looked at his friends. Then he took a deep breath and opened the door.

Ruth Rose slipped out just as Detective Reddy walked in.

"Hi, there," said Detective Reddy. He grinned at Dink and Josh. "Gee, you kids are clever. How'd you find the red-head with the video?"

Dink stared at the man in front of him. He couldn't believe it. Detective Reddy wasn't a detective at all. He was a bank robber! And he was standing in Dink's own living room!

"We were just lucky, I guess," Dink mumbled.

The man patted his mustache. "So where is it?"

Dink wouldn't let his eyes look at the lump under Josh's shirt. "Where's what?"

"The video. You called and said you had the video. So where is it?"

Dink's mind went blank. He didn't know what to say.

Think, Dink! he commanded himself.

Josh came to the rescue. "We hid the tape upstairs, remember, Dink?"

Dink stared at Josh. "Huh? Oh, yeah, now I remember." He grinned at the man. "We wanted to make sure no one saw it before we gave it to you."

"Come on, Dink." Josh headed for the stairs.

"It takes two of you to get one video?" the man said.

"Well...um...it's in my mother's room." Dink held up his front door key. "I'm the only one allowed to unlock her door."

Dink hurried up the stairs behind Josh. They ran into Dink's bedroom and shut the door.

Dink's guinea pig, Loretta, started squeaking and running around in her cage.

"Not now, Loretta," Dink said.

"Where'd Ruth Rose go?" said Josh.

"I can't believe she ditched us!"

Dink didn't answer. He paced back and forth in front of his bed. He tugged on his hair. He snapped his fingers nervously.

"Dink, stop, I'm getting dizzy," Josh said. "What're we gonna do?"

Dink stopped. "I don't know! We can't give him the video. He'll destroy it. Then nobody can prove anything! He'll get away scot-free. And he might even go after Lucky!"

"We have to catch him and hand him over to the cops," Josh said. "Do you have any rope? We'll jump him and tie him up!"

"I don't keep rope in my bedroom, Josh," Dink said. "Besides, he's bigger and stronger than us. He might even have a gun!"

"Need any help up there?" the man yelled.

Dink opened his door a crack. "No
thanks. We'll be right down."

Dink grabbed a soccer video from
his bookshelf and handed it to Josh.
"Let's give him this."

"But what happens when he finds

out it's not the real video?" Josh asked.

"I don't know. But we don't have any choice."

Josh pulled Lucky's video out of his shirt. He dropped it in Loretta's cage and covered it with shavings.

"Guard it, Loretta," he said.

They walked downstairs. Dink tried to smile.

"We found it!" he said.

Josh handed over the soccer video.

Just then the front door flew open. Ruth Rose was standing there with Officer Fallon and Officer Keene from the Green Lawn Police Department.

Dink was never so happy to see anyone.

"That's him!" Ruth Rose declared. She pointed at the man holding the videotape. "He robbed the Green Lawn bank!"

The officers stepped into the living room.

The man smiled. "I'm a private detective, officers," he said.

"Mind showing us some identification, sir?" said Officer Fallon.

The man patted his mustache. "I

don't have my wallet with me."

"You don't?" Officer Keene said. "Detectives are required to carry their identification at all times."

"Sure, and normally I do. But I left my wallet in the car. I'll get it and be right back."

"His mustache is fake!" Ruth Rose said, stepping in front of the officers. "And so is that wig!"

Everybody stared at the man.

Suddenly, he grabbed Ruth Rose and held her in front of him.

"Outta my way!" he yelled. "I'm leaving, and the girl's coming with me!"

Ruth Rose took a deep breath.

Then she let out the loudest scream of her life.

"AIIIIIIIIIEEEEEEEEE!"

Chapter
9

Josh, Dink, and the officers covered their ears.

"Ouch!" cried the bank robber.

He stumbled backward, clapping his hands over his ears.

The minute he let go of Ruth Rose, Officer Fallon grabbed him.

"It's all over, fella," Officer Fallon said. He snapped handcuffs on the man's wrists.

Officer Keene pulled off the thief's fake mustache and wig. Now the man looked just the way he did in the video. He had a shiny bald head and a surprised look on his face.

Officer Keene took him outside.

Officer Fallon put his hand on Ruth Rose's shoulder. "Ruth Rose, are you all right?"

Ruth Rose nodded. "I'm fine, Officer Fallon."

"So where's this videotape you told me about?"

Josh ran upstairs and got Lucky's video. He came back and slid it into the VCR. While they watched, Dink told Officer Fallon how it all happened.

Officer Fallon laughed. "Pretty clever of our thief. He hired you to find the video with his own face in it. If he got rid of the tape, no one could prove he was in that bank."

"He couldn't look for the tape himself," Ruth Rose explained. "The kid who taped him might have recognized him, like I did."

"How did you kids get hold of this video?" Officer Fallon asked.

Dink remembered their promise to Lucky. "We can't tell where we got it. We promised."

Officer Fallon smiled. "Well, whoever caught that guy on tape deserves a reward. Speaking of which, I believe you kids will be sharing a five-thousand-dollar reward from the bank."

"Five thousand dollars!" Josh jumped out of his seat. He and Dink did a little dance around the living room.

Officer Fallon laughed. "Ruth Rose here is a brave girl. She snuck over to her house and called the police station."

Ruth Rose turned her favorite shade of pink.

When Officer Fallon left, Ruth Rose did some math on Dink's calculator. "After we give Lucky his half, we'll each get $833.33," she said. "With a penny left over."

"We're rich!" said Josh. "Let's spend it!"

Dink laughed. "Mine's going into my savings account."

"Mine, too," Ruth Rose said. "I'm saving for a computer."

Josh slumped into a chair. "Yeah, you're right. My folks would kill me if I blew eight hundred bucks on pizza and ice cream."

On Monday, Dink, Josh, and Ruth Rose ran to the high school as soon as Green Lawn Elementary let out. They sat on a bench in front of the high school, out of breath.

"What did Lucky say when you told him he's getting half of five thousand dollars?" Josh asked.

"Nothing," Dink said, smiling. "I didn't tell him."

Just then the bell rang. A few seconds later, kids came streaming out of the high school.

"There he is!" Ruth Rose ran to meet Lucky O'Leary. She brought him over to the bench. He was smiling.

"Ruth Rose says you got paid. Did you bring my hundred and fifty?" he asked.

Dink shook his head sadly. "Not exactly."

"What do you mean, 'Not exactly'?"

The three friends burst out laughing.

"We don't have a hundred and fifty

dollars, but we do have this," said Dink.

He handed Lucky a check for $2,500.

Lucky's mouth and eyes popped open. "Twenty-five hundred bucks!" he yelled. "Where did *this* come from?"

"That's your half of the reward from the bank," Dink said. "We looked at your tape when we got home. Ruth Rose recognized the robber. He turned out to be the detective, only he wasn't really a detective. He was just pretending to be one so he could find you to get your video."

Lucky blinked. "So you guys nabbed him?"

"Yeah, right in Dink's house!" Josh said. "Ruth Rose snuck out and called the cops."

"It was exciting!" said Ruth Rose.

Lucky stared at his check again. He shook his head and grinned. "This is my lucky day. Now my mom can get the kids all their school stuff and have the car fixed."

"What about college?" Dink asked. "I thought that's what you were going to do with your money."

Lucky shook his head. "College is out for now. I'll have to work for a while till Mom and I can save more." Lucky looked at his check. "Maybe next year."

He shook hands with the three kids. "Anyway, thanks a lot for this check. I can't wait to see my mom's face when I give it to her!"

Dink watched Lucky walk away. Only he wasn't limping as much today.

"I wonder how many college courses Lucky could buy with my $833.33," he said.

Ruth Rose smiled at Dink. "I wonder how many college books he could buy with mine," she said.

Josh stared. "What? You're giving *your* money to Lucky? But you earned it!"

Dink shook his head. "No, we didn't. We just ran around talking to people. Lucky really earned the reward money."

"That's right," Ruth Rose said. "He's the one who caught the robber on videotape."

Dink and Ruth Rose started walking toward Main Street.

"Hey, where you guys going?" Josh yelled.

"To the bank," Dink said over his shoulder. "And then to Lucky's house."

Ruth Rose turned around and looked at Josh. "You coming with us?"

Josh grinned, then caught up with Dink and Ruth Rose. "I wonder how many college *meals* Lucky can buy with my $833.33," he said.

"Race you to the bank!" said Ruth
Rose.

And the three friends took off.

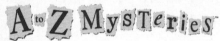

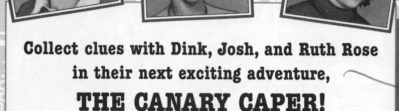

Collect clues with Dink, Josh, and Ruth Rose in their next exciting adventure,

THE CANARY CAPER!

"I think someone is stealing pets in Green Lawn," Ruth Rose said. "Two pets vanished on the same day!"

"Four pets," Officer Fallon said. He opened his drawer and pulled out a sheet of paper. "Four pets are missing from Green Lawn."

"Four?" Dink and Josh said together.

Officer Fallon nodded. "Thursday night I got a call from Dr. Pardue. His kids' rabbit wasn't in its cage. Later, Mrs. Gwynn called. It seems her parrot disappeared off her back porch."

"I was right!" Ruth Rose said, jumping to her feet. "There *is* a petnapper in town!"